Bethan Seaton lives in South Wales; she has thirteen nieces and nephews.

Bethan has worked as a healthcare administration assistant for 12 years; this is her first fictional children's novel.

In 2019, Bethan attended cognitive behavioural therapy. During therapy, she told her therapist she wanted to write a book and here is the proof that anything is possible.

BETHAN SEATON

BABY DINOSAUR

AUSTIN MACAULEY PUBLISHERS™

LONDON • CAMBRIDGE • NEW YORK • SHARJAH

A CIP catalogue record for this title is available from the British Library.

ISBN 9781398433199 (Paperback)
ISBN 9781398433205 (ePub e-book)

www.austinmacauley.com

First Published (2021)
Austin Macauley Publishers Ltd
25 Canada Square
Canary Wharf
London
E14 5LQ

To my grandparents, Robert Seaton, Joseph Gulwell and Doreen Gulwell, for the unconditional love and support you showed and gave me. Although you're not here to witness this, I know you would have been proud.

Thank you to all the people that believed in me when I didn't believe in myself and my therapist for helping me find myself.

Deep in the jungle lived a baby dinosaur. The baby dinosaur was very sad; he was lonely and had no friends. So one day, he said to mummy dinosaur, "Mummy, I'm going to look for some friends."

Mummy said, "OK, but be careful."

STOMP STOMP STOMP!
Off he went through the jungle.

A little time later, he came across a big tree that had some monkeys playing in it. He stopped and shouted up, "Hey monkeys, can I please play with you?"
The monkeys laughed. "HA HA HA HA! You can't play with us; we are monkeys that jump around trees and you are a dinosaur who doesn't even climb trees. HA HA HA HA HA!"

Baby dinosaur was very hurt and upset by what the monkeys said and continued walking.

After a little while, baby dinosaur came across some elephants, zebras and giraffes by a river.
He said, "Hey, may I please play with you?"
The elephants ignored baby dinosaur and walked the other way, the zebras just drank water out of the river without even stopping to look at baby dinosaur and the giraffes looked down and said, "We are giraffes, how do you suggest you play with us? We are far too tall for you."

By this point, baby dinosaur felt so upset that he had tears rolling down his face and decided to go home.

"Why? Why will nobody let me play with them?" he said aloud to himself as he was about to pass by a cave. Just then, a little voice in the shadow said, "Why are you sad, little dinosaur?"

As little dinosaur turned to the cave, he noticed a baby bear sat in the cave entrance.

The baby bear repeated the question, "Why are you so sad, baby dinosaur?"

"Oh, nobody will let me play with them because I can't climb trees or I'm too small," said baby dinosaur.

"I will play with you," said baby bear.

"Really? You will?" baby dinosaur said.

"Yes, why not? Just because you are a dinosaur, can't climb trees and you're small, it doesn't mean you are not fun to play with," said baby bear

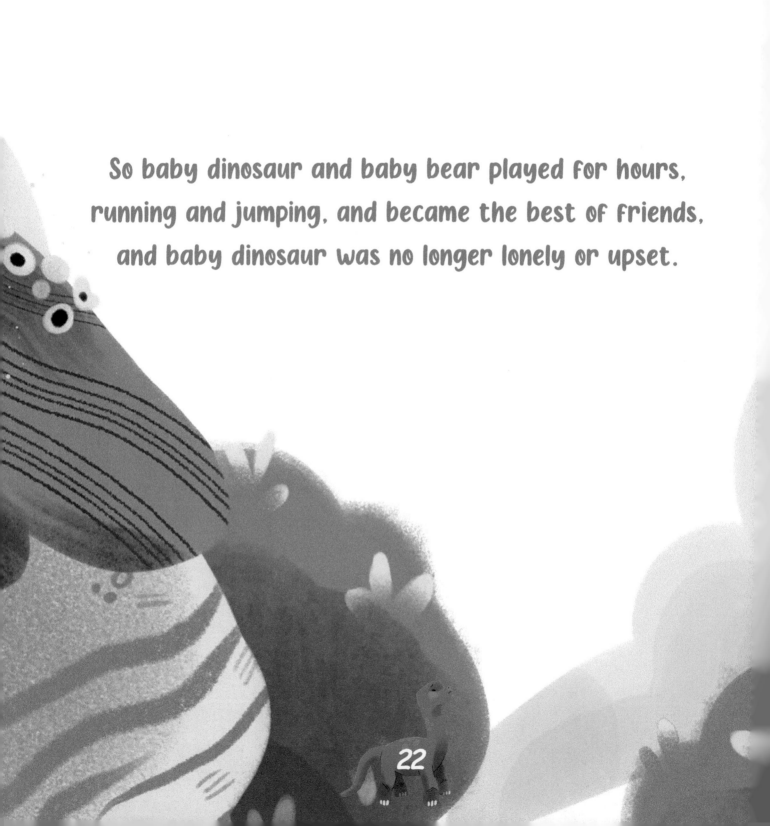

So baby dinosaur and baby bear played for hours, running and jumping, and became the best of friends, and baby dinosaur was no longer lonely or upset.

9 781398 433199